A Tudor Spy Story

UNDER THE ROSE:
A Tudor Spy Story

By Alan Childs

Illustrated by Stephen Millingen

ANGLIA *young* BOOKS

First published in 1991
by Anglia Young Books
Durhams Farmhouse
Ickleton
Saffron Walden, Essex CB10 1SR
Reprinted 1992

Reprinted 1996

Illustrations by Stephen Millingen

British Library Cataloguing-in-Publication Data

A catalogue record for this book is available from the British Library

ISBN 1 871173 11 6

Typeset in Palatino
and printed in Great Britain by
Ashford Colour Press, Gosport, Hampshire

To my mother and father

CHAPTER ONE

'Get up Crispin!' A soft leather shoe thrown across the room hit the side of the boy's ear.

'Crispin, get up. Master Thomas is coming.' Three sleepy figures were lying on the floor of the small shop and the youngest, Crispin, was directly in front of the door leading to the upper chambers. He just managed to scramble to his feet as the well-rounded form of Master Thomas Talbot burst through.

'You lazy scullions. Why is the fire still not lit? Lord save me from idle apprentices.'

The city churches were busy proclaiming the hour of five o'clock and the July daylight was already showing through cracks in the street shutters. The two older boys had leapt into action and were scurrying around collecting faggots and smaller twigs from the pile they had prepared the day before.

From upstairs the crying of young children was proof that the rest of Master Thomas's family was already awake.

'Pack the wood in carefully Robin, to spread the heat evenly.' Both older boys were now feeding the domed brick beehive oven with the dry wood, whilst Thomas muttered and mumbled his way round the candle-lit shop. He was never in a good humour at this time in the morning, and the boys had learnt to be careful. Robin, a tall skinny rake of a boy, was 14. His job was to strike the tinder and light the fire in the bakehouse oven.

'Luke, bring me a sack of wheat flour for the manchet bread, and a sack of rye flour also.'

Luke disappeared to the storeroom at the back. He was 13 and a strong lad, but his mind was too much on football and archery to make a good baker. He lived for the apprentices' rough and tumble games, with a hundred a side. Last Shrove Tuesday the injuries were dreadful but he was not put off.

'Shall I put the wheat flour near the trough Master Thomas?'

'Yes, boy. Measure out the usual amount for our first baking and don't take all day.'

Once a week, Master Thomas and the three boys took the cart to the mills on Finsbury Fields, just north of the city, and brought back sufficient flour for a week's baking. The boys enjoyed watching the archers practising in the Finsbury Butts and always hoped to beg a turn if Thomas was gossiping.

Robin struck the spark and a handful of straw was soon alight; the sticks in the oven crackled. The iron door was closed when the twigs and branches were well lit.

Thomas's wife Sarah entered the shop wearing her morning work gown and a pretty woollen kirtle. She was a plump good-natured woman who treated all the apprentices like sons.

Master Crispin,' she called, 'change the rushes on the shop floor if you please and don't forget to scatter the wormwood, for you know the saying, Where chamber is swept and wormwood is strown . . .'

In chorus the three boys finished it off for her, 'No flea for his life dare abide to be known.' They had heard it often.

'Are you mocking me you ragamuffins!' But Mistress Sarah took their teasing in good spirit and they were all laughing. Crispin still turned up his nose at the job. He didn't like the smell of wormwood at all, especially sleeping on top of it.

'Also Master Crispin, I believe 'tis your turn to go to Cheapside Market. I shall need more milk for my cheese-making, some rue and rosemary from the herb-seller, and some oranges and cloves for pomanders.'

Master Thomas had been half listening as he weighed out the rye flour from the sack.

'Oh no wife, are you going to make our lives a misery again by your worries over the plague?' Thomas's eyes twinkled as he mocked his wife.

'But Thomas there are rumours . . .'

'Rumours of the plague have spread like fire in thatch every summer we have lived in London, and we are still alive.'

'You may mock me, but this summer the air smells fouler than ever before. I shall protect our children and you can catch the plague if you wish.'

Sarah had heard that the herb rue spread on the windowsills and a sprig of rosemary burnt at night-time would protect them from the bad air that the doctors said carried the plague.

Robin was now boulting the wheat flour through a piece

of coarse linen to get rid of the bran and sweeping it into a pile, using a goosewing. The other boys were putting out the trenchers on the table and filling leather mugs with ale. Mistress Sarah brought in a round flat cheese, a pot of honey and a piece of ham for Thomas, and while Robin finished his work the others breakfasted on yesterday's unsold loaves and the tangy cheese. The young children were fed upstairs.

'Watch where the flour is falling Master Robin. I be not made of money.' The master baker was always chiding the boys for their wastefulness.

When all, including Robin, had eaten, Luke and Crispin collected up the sieved flour and placed it in a wooden trough for Master Thomas to add the salt, yeast and water. Kneading the dough was the hardest job. Thomas worked fast, pushing and stretching. When the dough was ready, the apprentices weighed the amount for each loaf and shaped the rounds for manchet bread, the finest quality. They pricked the top and left it to rise.

'Don't forget my stamp on every loaf boys, or the Baker's Company will be after my blood.'

'Why does it matter so much?' Crispin could never understand the fuss made about stamping loaves with the marks of the bakers.

'Because Crispin, everyone is not as honest as I am. That mark means the loaf is guaranteed full weight. I heard a story the other day about a baker who had a small trapdoor in the table where the loaves were being made and a little apprentice, a bit smaller than you, reached through and cut dough off the bottom of the weighed loaves. This was all free bread for the baker and his family. I am glad to say he was caught.'

The fire had been re-stoked and for half an hour the four of them worked in silence.

'See if the oven's hot enough Master Luke.' The boy opened the door and turned his face away from the heat. The bricks inside the dome were glowing. Quickly the fire was raked out and before heat could be lost the baker loaded the loaves onto the flat end of the long wooden peel and pushed them into the heat at the back of the oven.

'Four dozen loaves loaded boys. Slam the door shut, then get some mud from the yard Master Crispin.' Crispin did so and plastered the mud round the gaps in the door to seal in the heat. The floor was swept clean of flour and ashes and the table and trough wiped thoroughly.

'Shall I open the shutters Master Thomas?'

'Yes Luke, we shall soon have bread for London.'

The front of the shop was formed of hinged shutters. Luke opened these and they made a flat surface sticking out into the street from which the customers could be served.

Crispin was now free to go out on Mistress Sarah's errand whilst his fellow apprentices prepared the next batch of bread. He pulled on his leather jerkin and flat woollen cap and walked outside.

Although still early in the morning, Bread Street was full of noise and bustle. Apprentices were calling to each other and carts were rumbling over the cobbles bringing milk and vegetables into Cheapside market from the villages around the city. The stench in the street was dreadful. Though he had lived in London for almost all of his eleven and a half years, still Crispin could not get used to it. It had been a hot summer and the smell was worse than ever. He stepped over the piles of rubbish which caused the problem and kept a wary eye on the upper windows of the houses as he walked. Being showered with night slops from the bed chambers was not a good way to start the day!

From Bread Street he entered the thriving street named Cheapside, 'the Cheape' the Londoners called it, where all the countryfolk set up their stalls. From every direction he was being pressed to buy:

'Salt, fine white salt', 'Juniper, sweet juniper', 'New brooms, green brooms', 'Very fine writing ink', 'Venice glasses', 'Hot fine oatcake', 'Cherries, ripe cherries' and this morning the street cry that always made Crispin laugh, 'Sweep, chimney sweep masters, From the bottom to the top, Then shall no soot fall in your porridge pot.'

The London church bells added their voice to the cacophony of sound and Crispin stopped to listen. He loved this time of the morning, especially here in Cheapside.

He passed the ancient 'Eleanor' Cross, so recently attacked and defaced, much to Queen Elizabeth's annoyance. Certain citizens had found its gildings too Catholic and too potent a reminder of the bad old days of the late Queen Mary. He passed The Conduit where water-carriers filled their tall containers. The water came in lead pipes all the way from Paddington Heights.

Suddenly there was a pushing from behind him.

'Make passage there.' Crispin was almost knocked over by a tall figure running along the road, one of the 'Watch' who had the impossible task of keeping law and order in that violent city. No-one was really safe and it was said that even the young Queen was in constant danger.

'Make passage I say.' Crispin followed at a trot to where a small crowd had gathered round a figure lying on the ground, half slumped against the wall of the Pope's Head tavern. He seemed to be a beggar. They were a common enough sight in the city and were tormented by ordinary citizens. The stocks and pillory were always good for entertainment. Crispin noted the hole in the man's right ear, the painful proof of a hot iron that many a beggar carried to his grave.

'Get up fellow.' The watchman kicked his side hard.

'He can't get up. He's ill. Probably got the plague,' shouted someone. At this, the inquisitive crowd surged back a pace, not wishing to touch the man.

'He's a soap eater, he's foaming at the mouth,' laughed the tight-bellied inn-keeper of the tavern. Crispin had heard of this trick of faking madness.

The watchman pulled the man forward, away from the jostling crowd of boys and street sellers. A wet, red patch was staining the back of the torn cloak. The watchman let go of him and the beggar fell back.

'He's been stabbed,' shouted someone from the crowd. Immediately there was a push forward again, and Crispin was at the front, too close now to the dying man. Around him the pushers and shovers were arguing and no-one was looking down any more. Crispin just wanted to get away but for one moment his eyes caught the eyes of the beggar. He felt a light touch on his arm and then something pressing his open palm . When the beggar released his hold Crispin found he was clutching a piece of parchment.

'Get a litter for him,' someone suggested.

'All he needs is a coffin.' The watchman's voice sounded flat and indifferent. No-one seemed surprised or concerned and everyone dispersed quickly, leaving him to deal with the body. Life was cheap and death commonplace in the streets of the city.

Crispin stood up, still clutching the piece of parchment, and looked round to see if anyone had noticed. There had been a desperate plea in the beggar's face, but what was Crispin supposed to do?

Quickly he tucked the parchment inside his cap and turned away to find the herb-seller. As he moved off, a pair of eyes followed him. From the deep shadows beneath the overhanging upper storey of the chandler's shop opposite the tavern, a street seller was watching everything. He was dressed in a dull blue doublet, slashed in the modern fashion and had a small pointed black beard. He walked along the side of the wide street exactly opposite the boy but still keeping in the shadows of the houses. He carried a tray of quills and ink and paper, but his clothes were not the clothes of a trader. When Crispin bent to stroke a stray dog the man stopped. When the boy quickened his pace the man hurried also. When Crispin made his purchases from the stalls and gossiped to the familiar vendors, the man stopped and pretended interest in the shop nearest to him.

Walking back down Bread Street, the man was only a few paces behind him. Outside Thomas's shop Crispin stopped. The first batch of quartern loaves was on display and the delicious smell drifted into the street. As the boy entered the door the man's eyes noted everything.

'Make speedy return when you shall be sent on your Masters' and Mistresses' business.' Wasn't this one of the apprentices' rules? Crispin expected a cuff round the ear for taking so long on a simple errand. Luke was already hard at work on the next trough of dough and Robin was preparing a tray of bread to deliver. They both jeered at him for shirking. But Master Thomas was not able to display his temper in the usual way, for standing in the dim light at the back of the shop was a tall figure dressed in a fur-lined gown and wearing a square black cap above his shaven face.

'Crispin, come over here, I want you to meet Master John Kyme.' The stranger inclined his head slightly to greet the boy and smiled, putting the apprentice at his ease. Crispin was about to take off his cap when he remembered the piece of parchment and decided that manners must take second place.

'Master Kyme has come here with a very generous proposal Crispin. It seems that despite the undoubted laziness of all my apprentices, he's prepared to offer one of you the chance of bettering yourself . . .' The stranger now broke into the conversation.

'As your Master knows, I work in the household of a very important man whose position is close to the Queen herself. He has his London house quite near here, and for reasons I cannot confide at present, he has need of a number of additional servants. In particular he has need of an intelligent . . .' here the man stopped a moment and smiled, 'willing and hard-working boy to help in the kitchen. A degree of skill at baking would not go amiss. As your Master rightly says, it is a chance that comes not a boy's way but once in a lifetime. Your Master has proposed that you might be suited to such a job, so what say you boy?'

Crispin looked across at the grinning faces of Luke and Robin. The boy was at a loss for words. He was still shaken from the scene he had witnesssed in the street and puzzled by the strange parchment inside his cap. Since his real parents had died he had known nothing but life with Thomas and Sarah. Now they were suggesting he should leave them. His world was being rocked.

'Well, what is your reply boy?' Master Kyme had taken a step nearer to Crispin and was again smiling at the boy's dazed look. 'He is not dumb I take it Master Talbot!'

'Speak up boy,' said Thomas, 'what do you say?'

'If my Master thinks I can serve in this way sir, then I must gladly accept.' Crispin picked the words which he felt Master Thomas would approve and it seemed as if someone else were speaking them.

'Good, well said boy. Now pack your belongings right away. I shall send a servant to direct you to the house in Aldersgate later this day. My thanks then Master Talbot. Fare you well.' He swept out of the door and was gone.

CHAPTER TWO

In the little garret under the roof Crispin looked at the sad collection of objects before him. His total worldly possessions did not amount to much when they were spread out on the floor. His best doublet and trunk hose with a fine shirt – all made by Mistress Sarah, and hardly worn. The game of Nine Men's Morris that Master Thomas had made for his tenth birthday, the little wooden pegs painted red and white like the rose of the Tudors. The lucky silver groat that he had won wrestling last August at Bartholomew's Fair, four pennies in one coin and never to be spent unless he was in distress. And there, although he could not read it was his one book, a small bible with his Mother's name written in a spidery hand inside the front cover, Anne Meryman Her Book, and then some strange numbers that he could not understand, MDXLVII. This of all was his proudest possession. And now, as his lopsided cap reminded him, he had one other possession that he was not sure he wanted to own. He took out the piece of parchment and looked at the writing that meant nothing to him. The only thing about it that he could understand was the scribbled sign on the outside, the sign of a rose.

'Crispin!' Thomas's voice bellowed up the stairs startling him from his day-dream, 'how long does it take you to get your things in a bundle? Get down here now boy. We are waiting.'

Down the stairs he ran, his belongings in a cloth bundle over his shoulder. When he hurtled through the door into the shop he found a servant waiting there, dressed in the grey 'marbled' livery of his master, and everyone else waiting to say goodbye. Robin and Luke just stood there awkwardly. Mistress Sarah had tears in her eyes.

'Is this the pipkin of trouble for Master Kyme?' said the servant. Thomas knew the man well.

'Yes, one less mouth to feed. I wish I could get rid of the other two as easily. You wouldn't care to take all three?'

Crispin did not know whether to laugh or cry. He was glad the boys had got on with their work and that the men were talking when Sarah put her arm round his shoulder and whispered close to his ear,

'Crispin you know you will have a home with us whenever you need it. We promised your dear Mother and . . . Oh Lord save me, I'm a silly old woman upsetting myself and you as well.' She turned to go upstairs, tears streaming down her face. Crispin rubbed his eyes with his shirt sleeve.

'Come young Master' said the servant, 'goodbyes are no things for men to deal with.' They walked the whole length of Bread Street past the jeers and whistles of some of the other bakers' apprentices, then into Cheapside, past Mary le Bow Church and past the Pope's Head Tavern again that day. His eyes were drawn to the spot where the beggar had lain. Nothing but a stain on the ground was evidence that a killing had happened. He wondered where the body had been taken. Thrown into a pauper's grave with none of the fine church words to send him on his way?

'My name's Francis Wyatt, young Master. What do I call you?'

'Crispin Meryman.'

'Crispin! You should have been a shoemaker not a baker,' laughed the man.

'I suppose I should,' Crispin laughed back. He had been called Crispin because his birthday had fallen on the saint's day, October 25th. St. Crispin was the patron saint of shoemakers.

Francis talked non-stop as they walked through the back streets to Aldersgate. He called out to shopkeepers and to servants in their different liveries. In between all of this he gave Crispin a few words of advice:

'Keep on the right side of Mistress Wells boy. She's the housekeeper at Aldersgate and she rules the household. Work hard, hold your tongue and you will fare well.'

When Francis and his young charge were nearing Sir William's house something happened that afterwards puzzled Crispin. It seemed that as he was walking, someone's foot caught his ankle intentionally from behind. Before he knew it he was sprawling in the muddy road. Francis was unaware of this and walked on, still talking. Several arms went down to help, but one man in particular seemed anxious about the boy.

'How clumsy of me young fellow. I fear it may have been my fault that your stockings and shirt are now so muddy and your cap has ended in a puddle.' The man picked up the cap as Crispin scrambled to his feet and seemed for a brief moment to turn it rather deliberately in his hand. His manner was friendly, and yet unnerving to the boy for it was unusual for a gentleman of his sort to bother with a mere apprentice boy. The bearded face stooped close to Crispin and their eyes met.

'Allow me to give you half a groat for my carelessness boy.' He thrust the coin into the boy's hand from the pouch on his blue doublet.

'Are you apprenticed near here?'

'No sir, I am this day starting in the service of Sir William Petre.' The man seemed to lose himself in thought before he replied.

'Sir William indeed. His house is in Aldersgate. I know it well. I see you have your worldly belongings tied in that bundle . . .' The man said no more because by now Francis had retraced his steps and was heading for Crispin with a worried look on his face. When Crispin explained what had happened, the gentleman was nowhere to be seen.

'Worth a tumble in the mud for two pennies,' Francis laughed.'Now come quickly Crispin. Master Kyme will think I have gone off to watch the bear-baiting, or lost my way in a tavern more like!'

· · · · ·

Aldersgate Street was an area of rich houses and Crispin's eyes grew wide as he neared his new home.

'Your new master is an important man Crispin. I hope you realise that. Sir William has been close to the throne since old Henry's days. He is a kind master, but careful with his pennies, so watch that you be not wasteful.'

Crispin chuckled. 'Master Thomas was just the same.'

They passed the imposing front of the house and went

through a side gate into a lovely garden, set with lawns and fruit trees. There was the sound of horses from the stables. To Crispin who had never in his life been into such a garden it was like leaving London and entering the country. Even the air smelt cleaner.

They went through a door, along a stone-flagged passageway and into a large kitchen. Seated at a table was a grey-haired white-bonneted lady surrounded by skillets and spoons and spices. The hearth to her right had a blazing fire and all round the room were bowls of food in various stages of preparation yet no other servant was to be seen.

'Mistress Wells.This is Crispin, the new kitchen boy, somewhat muddy from a fall in the street.' Francis retreated, leaving Crispin feeling very uncomfortable.

'Gracious Heavens! What have you been doing?'

Crispin felt unequal to the task of explaining to her what had really happened but was just about to attempt it when Mistress Wells called out quite loudly,

'Hannah, come in here girl.'

A door at the far end of the kitchen opened and someone peeped round the door. A girl of about Crispin's age came into the room. He looked at her red hair and freckled grinning face, and could not but grin back.

'Hannah, take this street urchin to the small chamber by my master's study. Look in the chest of spare clothes and find him a shirt and hose and perhaps a belt and cap as well. Then take him to the servants' chambers so he can change his muddy clothes. And Master Crispin, before you do that, put your head under the pump and wash your hands.'

Hannah showed Crispin the pump and then escorted him to the top of the house past rooms the like of which Crispin had never seen.

'Look in there Crispin.' Hannah had pushed open an oak panelled door into the most beautiful room. The large bed was curtained with red and white silk, and on the walls were tapestries showing pictures of sheep and red flowers.

'That's my master's bed-chamber.' Hannah was proud to show Crispin the wonders of the house. Even the straw mattresses in the servants' rooms were luxury after sleeping on Thomas's shop floor.

When Crispin reappeared for Mistress Wells' inspection he looked a different boy in his gleaming white shirt and green hose. So much had happened to him that day that he had quite forgotten he had missed a meal. Mistress Wells led him to the servants lodgings for his supper. A number of adult servants were already eating, but apart from Francis who beckoned him to sit beside him, no-one seemed interested. Comings and goings and new faces were part of everyday life in Sir William's house. Some days they ate there but often they were given a penny to find their own food in one of the local taverns or cookhouses. It depended whether Sir William was at the palace with the Queen. Their lives varied from day to day. Some of the servants had to accompany Sir William when he needed escorting by river, finding him a boat at Paul's Wharf and waiting for him at Whitehall Palace. It would often be after midnight when they returned, carrying his boxes of papers.

At the end of that long day Crispin was trying to sleep. He found his mind running back to the beggar's staring eyes. What did he want him to do? Trying not to disturb the other sleepers in the room, Crispin pulled his bundle towards him and felt for the rolled-up parchment. He looked at the strange writing, willing its secret to reveal itself. He felt in his heart that it was important. Perhaps it was what the beggar had been killed for. A shudder ran down his back. He felt very much alone, cut off from the life he had known and not knowing who to trust. But before exhaustion overtook him and his body forced his mind to stop working he had come to a decision. He would tell Hannah the secret. He needed someone on his side, but also he would ask Francis where he could get the letter read. Surely a stranger reading it wouldn't matter?

· · · · ·

Not far from where Crispin lay, in a room in the Swan Tavern a gentleman sat staring into the fire. The wine in the glass beside him was untouched. His mind was trapped in a problem that was bothering him. He was still deep in thought when the night watchman along Aldersgate Street called 'Twelve o'clock, look well to your locks.' And strangely, it was the beggar's face that also haunted him, and kept him from sleep.

CHAPTER THREE

Crispin's first morning at Aldersgate passed off well. The servants here arose at six of the clock so he enjoyed the luxury of one extra hour's sleep. He was asked to help in the bakery and the old baker was pleased with him.

'You have done well boy, I shall tell Master Kyme'. 'Tis true that once or twice Crispin had to bite his tongue when he was about to say 'Master Thomas doesn't do it like that', but the old man was relieved to have a boy who seemed to know what he was doing.

For the rest of the morning Crispin roasted in the heat of the kitchen, running hither and thither and trying not to make too many mistakes. Venison with gingered vinegar; pork served with pease pudding and blancmange; herrings in mustard sauce; Umbles Pie for the servants – made of the less expensive meats; plum porridge for the pudding. Such dishes Crispin was meeting for the first time, except for the pease pudding which Sarah often made. The rye bread, baked for the servants, Crispin thought very inferior stuff. He had been spoiled by working in a bakery.

Dinner was at 11 o'clock and after Crispin had helped wash all the trenchers the cook allowed him a few minutes rest in the sunshine of the garden. He found Francis sitting on a barrel outside the stable. Like most apprentices Crispin had developed a taste for ale and Francis was enjoying a tankard of beer, too bitter for the boys and women.

Crispin seized his chance to ask Francis about the matter that was troubling him.

'Francis, you don't know where I might go if I wanted a letter . . . written?'

Francis scratched his stubbly chin.

'A letter written you say.' His face brightened. 'Well it would like as not cost you a penny or two, but they do say that the cathedral is the place.'

'St.Paul's Cathedral?'

'Yes, though whether the scriveners are still there with no roof on the poor old church, I know not.'

Crispin had not yet seen it, but the whole city had been alive with the story of the steeple being struck by lightning and the roof burning – just a month ago.

'What are these scriv . . . ?'

'Scriveners. Scribes young master. Learned men who earn their money by writing documents for the likes of you and me who cannot do so themselves. I am certain you will find the answer to your problem there.'

'Thank you Francis. When do you think I might be able to go?'

'Well I hear that Master Kyme is returning with Sir William this night, then we shall be busy again. If you were to vanish for an hour or so this afternoon, I could probably find a reason.'

'Francis, could you find a reason for Hannah to vanish as well?'

· · · · ·

Early that afternoon Crispin plucked up courage to confide in Hannah. He felt certain he could trust her.

'You saw a beggar being killed!' she said with horror in her voice.

'Well I didn't see him being stabbed but I saw him die, and just before he died, he gave me this.'

Hannah and Crispin were sitting under the apple trees near the high brick wall which divided Sir William's land from his neighbour's mansion. Hannah picked up the piece of parchment and unrolled it.

'What can it mean?'

'It seemed as if he wanted me to do something with it, but I don't know what. I have to find out what it says.'

'What about Francis, wouldn't he . . . ?'

Crispin cut in, 'No I don't think so. I would feel happier with a stranger, and besides I might need a copy. Crispin told her about St. Paul's Cathedral. The garden was empty. The older servants had little to do and the only sounds were coming from the stables. The two horsekeepers were making use of Sir William's absence to get the saddles and bridles in good condition and to groom the horses.

'Hannah, would you keep the parchment instead of me?'

'Yes, but why . . . ?'

'I just think it's safer if I am not carrying it.'

They slipped quietly out of the gate to the street, past the Swan Tavern where in a front chamber facing the street two men were in heated conversation; the one, the man with the blue doublet, the other a swarthy-skinned Spaniard. Despite the children's speed and stealth, their movement along Aldersgate Street did not pass unnoticed.

They walked through the gate back inside the city wall and along St Martins. When old Thomas had given the apprentices time to themselves Crispin loved to explore the bustling city, from the tall-masted merchant ships in the docks to the wonders of London Bridge with its amazing Nonesuch House, and the gruesome remains of traitors over the gateway. The children threaded their way through the noisy crowds towards the Cathedral; along Paternoster Row where the rosary makers worked, a trade out of favour these days.

'Are your parents alive Crispin?'

'No my mother died of the plague and my father – well my father was killed.'

'Was he a soldier?'

'In a way he was.' Crispin never knew whether to tell people that his father had been a follower of a Norwich rebel by the name of Robert Kett and that the leader had ended up being hanged drawn and quartered. His father had died of wounds he received fighting for Robert Kett and the people of Norfolk.

'My parents are both dead too,' said Hannah, 'but I have an aunt in Moorgate, quite near to Sir William's house, the next gate but one along London Wall.

When they came within sight of the cathedral it was quite a shock, for very little of the roof remained. Blackened stones were scattered around and half-burnt timbers lay piled one upon the other. Most of the nave was open to the sky. The tower still stood, but without its steeple. People had said it was like a torch flaming, the night the lightning struck.

Inside, it reminded Crispin of Cheapside market more than a church. Despite the lack of a roof the cathedral was full of a noisy bustling crowd. It was still used as a short-cut for traders passing from one side of the city to the other so despite the law forbidding it, fishmongers crossed the floor carrying boxes of fish on their heads and barrels were rolled across the nave. Even animals were driven across the cathedral floor.

Crispin and Hannah had little problem in finding the scriveners. There was a whole row of them along 'Paul's Walk', with their movable stalls. Some were busily writing already, their quills scratching the parchment.

At one such stall sat a bald-headed rosy-cheeked man, dressed in a grey gown with a small ruff framing his head. He was leaning back against the wall and watching the world pass before him. His pen was dancing in his hand as if in time to some unheard music. He noticed the children's hesitancy.

'Good morrow young Master, young Mistress. Can I be of help to you? Master Gilbert Taverner at your service – scribe, scholar and former tutor to the great, now trying to earn my crust of bread in this stricken edifice.'

Hannah and Crispin exchanged glances. The man beamed as if reading their thoughts.

'No I am not a mountebank, neither am I a rogue. For two pennies I can pen you the finest letter your heart can desire. Young sir, this maiden is your sweetheart? You are running away to become betrothed and wish me to pen a letter to your cruel parents who are trying to keep you apart?

Hannah giggled and blushed. Crispin felt a tinge come over his own face.

'No that is not so, sir but I think you may be able to help me.'

'Anything, just instruct me. My pen is at your command.'

Hannah turned away from the man so that she could modestly remove the parchment from where she had hidden it, and gave it to Crispin.

'I should like you to read this parchment for me please. It . . . was given to me . . . by a friend . . . and I cannot read.'

The man took it and unrolled it, using two ink-holders to support the edges and to keep it flat. His eyes ran over the words and a puzzled expression creased his forehead.

'You were given the document, by a friend you say?'

'Yes.'

The man was silent for a few moments longer and both Crispin and Hannah waited for some sign that he could understand it.

'Your friend has given you what appears to be a list of

names and a message. I will read it to you from the beginning. The outside is marked thus with the sign of a rose and the words 'To Whit', a strange address to be sure, almost as if it was not finished. Inside it reads, 'Have a care for St James the Great may yet throw England into confusion. A progress may be stopped short when she who progresses is taken from her seat. The House in the Strand is at the heart of this affair and those named must needs be watched.' Then there follows a list of ten or so names.'

The man looked at the children and shrugged his shoulders.

'It means nothing to me. Perhaps St. James the Great is the name of a church. There are so many churches in the city. I know not all of them.

'Why is there a scribbled rose on the outside?' Hannah asked.

The man thought for a few seconds and then beamed again at them.

'Come with me. I think that's the easy part.'

He took them to the other end of the cathedral at such a pace that they had to run to keep up with him. They came to what looked like a small wooden walled room. He opened the door and inside was a simple seat with a kind of window leading to another box on the other side, except the window was blocked by a curtain.

'This box is what is called a confessional,' the man explained.' What is spoken in here is a secret between the person confessing and the priest on the other side. Now look up.'

The children did so and there on the ceiling was a carved wooden rose.

'Do you see the rose. That's a sign of secrecy. The words are spoken under the rose.'

Crispin looked again at the parchment the man was holding and the very definite rose that had been drawn. 'Under the rose', a sign of secrecy.

'Shall I copy the parchment out for you in an easier hand to read young master?'

Crispin agreed, knowing that the hand would make no difference to his reading it, but a copy could be useful. The job was soon completed and sand shaken over the ink to dry it. Crispin paid the scrivener the two pennies and he wished them well. Hannah took both sheets.

After the shadows of the cathedral the outside air seemed warm. They walked through St. Paul's churchyard with its line of booksellers and its throng of fine dandies passing their time in being seen. A little way along and Hannah suddenly realized that Crispin was with her no longer. He had disappeared.

CHAPTER FOUR

At first Hannah thought that Crispin was playing some game with her. She heard a drum banging outside an inn and wondered if he had sneaked in to watch the strolling actors in the innyard. She was angry with him, and started back towards the cathedral. She almost bumped into a hat seller with his hats piled one above the other on his head. Just before she reached St. Paul's churchyard for the second time she noticed a commotion in a tiny alleyway off the main street. A figure was on the ground and one or two shopkeepers and traders were gathered round. At first she didn't realise it was Crispin, but as she got close enough to see the colour of his hose she screamed and ran forward. He was lying semi-conscious near a cart and a countrywoman with a scarf round her mouth was wiping his face with a cloth soaked in water.

'Crispin, what's happened!' Hannah pushed her way through and the others moved back when they saw she knew him.

'Is he your brother Mistress?'

'No, we are servants, but I was walking with him just a minute past.'

'Looks to me as if a cutpurse has had a go at him.' An elderly farmer had been helping Crispin to sit up against the wheel of his cart. 'Can't see why anyone would want to rob a lad of his age. You should have called 'clubs' boy. All the 'prentices would have had him then.'

Crispin moved a little and started to come round. His

29

shirt was torn and the little purse on his belt had been ripped away and lay there in the dirt, the few coins still scattered beside it.

'Can you help me up Hannah, I'm all right.' Someone had brought him a mug of water. He had a cut over one eye where something had caught the skin. The woman dabbed at the drops of blood with the wet cloth.

A few minutes more and the blood-stained victim was on his feet, thanking those who had helped him. He said nothing more about it until he and Hannah were again walking towards Aldersgate.

'What happened Crispin?'

'I was attacked, that's what happened. And not just attacked but searched as well.'

'Searched! In Heaven's name why?'

'It wasn't a normal cutpurse Hannah. He didn't even take the money. I am certain now that he was looking for that parchment. The list of names must be something important.'

'Perhaps he was a friend of the old beggar.

'More like he was one of those who killed him for the list.

'But how could they guess that you had it? And how could they have followed you without us knowing? Did you see what the man was like Crispin?'

'I only saw his face for a second. It was dark, as if he was foreign.'

'Not a lot to help us. Come on, we'd better hurry back. Master Francis may be having trouble explaining our absence.

When they eventually reached Aldersgate and slipped in through the garden entrance the house was still quiet. Francis was talking to the horsekeepers outside the stable and he beckoned to them.

'What in the Devil's name has happened to you Master Crispin? You haven't been brawling, or playing football with those rough bakers' apprentices. A twinkle in his eye turned to a look of concern when he saw the cut and the state of Crispin's clothes. They had made up their mind that they should not say too much.

'He tripped over a barrel he was trying to jump. That will teach him to be clever.'

● ● ● ● ●

The church of St. Anne-in-the-Willows in Aldersgate had just struck the hour of six, and Crispin and Hannah were busily counting and sorting candles which had arrived that afternoon from the chandler's. They were in a little storeroom near the dry larder. Hannah was displaying her knowledge.

'These heaviest candles are 4 to the lb,' she explained. 'They are placed in the big candlesticks along the gallery. The next are 6 to the lb, and the smallest such as light us to our bed-chambers are 8 to the lb. My aunt makes her own candles. It's a horrible smelly job.'

Crispin had sometimes bought candles for Mistress Sarah from the shop in Cheapside, beeswax for special

occasions, costing more but smelling sweeter. They had almost finished their job when they heard voices. The main door of the house opened and closed.

'Quick Crispin, look very busy, that's Master Kyme and probably Sir William.' Sir William had indeed returned, walking with Master Kyme from the river. The food prepared earlier was ready in the ovens and John Kyme bustled through to inform the cook that their Master would eat. The children peeped from the storeroom and caught sight of his gown crossing the passageway near the kitchen.

It was an hour later that Crispin, together with all the indoor servants, was summoned by Mistress Wells to attend in the Gallery – the long panelled room close to Sir William's study. There were nine or ten servants present in a line along one wall of the room, with the children at the end. Through the windows they could see the comings and goings in Aldersgate. One or two of the houses opposite had already closed their shutters.

The door opened at the end of the gallery and Master Kyme came into the room. Behind him was a man of medium build, dressed in a gown of fine black damask and with rich lace at his neck and cuffs. Around his shoulders was a medallion of office and on his chin a neat well-groomed beard. He walked slowly with a slight stoop to his gait.

Crispin saw that the servants bowed or curtsied as he walked in front of them and he bowed as well as he could. Sir William Petre was one of the most important men in the Queen's government. He was a clever lawyer who had managed to stay at the very centre of affairs for a great many years. He had held high office under Queen

Elizabeth's father Henry, steering a course through the troubles of the break with Rome. He continued under the boy king Edward, when England could have seen another civil war. He even survived under Elizabeth's half-sister 'Bloody Mary'. When many another statesman toppled, Sir William rode the bucking horse of government and stayed in the saddle. This was the man who had the cares of the country on his shoulders, and Crispin was in his service.

Sir William spoke in a soft deliberate voice choosing the words so it seemed as if every one was weighed carefully.

'What I am about to say to you all must remain for the moment a secret within these walls.' There was a murmur of assent from the adults. 'Tomorrow morning, apart from Mistress Wells and the outdoor servants, all of you will be taken by stage-waggon to Ingatestone Hall.' There were exchanged looks and glances. 'Many of you have been in my service for some time and will know that because of my office it is my duty,' he corrected himself, 'indeed my pleasure, to entertain those of importance in the affairs of this country. On the 19th of this month, in three days time, Ingatestone Hall is to be honoured by a very special guest and it is your privilege to help my servants at Ingatestone prepare for that visit.'

A question was on Hannah's lips as she mouthed something to Crispin. Sir William continued:

'Our guest is to be Her Gracious Majesty Queen Elizabeth.' There was a gasp from the servants and Sir William continued. 'The Queen is to honour us on the first stage of her summer Progress this year in the Eastern Counties. There will be much to do and much for you to see. I will leave Master Kyme now to explain to you the arrangements for the morrow. I bid you all goodnight.'

Turning suddenly, Sir William walked back to his study and the door closed.

The servants could not restrain themselves and a buzz of excited voices filled the gallery.

Before they went to their chambers Hannah and Crispin had a serious talk. The attack that day had worried them both. They were convinced that while they had the parchment they would be in danger. They had to show it to someone. Crispin suddenly came to a decision.

'I'm going to take it to Master Kyme. I'm sure I can trust him.'

'What *now* Crispin, you must be mad! It's late and he's very very busy. He'll send you away with a flea in your ear, I'm certain of that.'

But instead of taking the attic stairs to the servants chambers Crispin took the corridor which he knew led to John Kyme's chamber. The candles flickered in their holders as he stood staring at the outside of the oak door. Closing his eyes he summoned up courage to knock.

'Come inside,' called a voice and Crispin opened the door and went in.

CHAPTER FIVE

As soon as possible the next morning Hannah eagerly sought out Crispin to ask what had happened.

'Master Kyme questioned me about every detail including that stranger in the blue doublet who tripped me up. He said he felt certain the attack near the cathedral was because of the parchment.

'What is he going to do about it?'

'He's kept the parchment and the copy. He said he would see me about it later, probably at Ingatestone.'

The children were relieved to be rid of the parchment but the feeling of danger still lay over their heads. Luckily the next few hours passed in a breathless whirl of activity. Chests had to be packed with spoons and knives, pewter and silver plate, wooden trenchers for the extra servants, bed coverings and straw mattresses. Even the best wall hangings were taken from Aldersgate, to decorate the Queen's chambers.

The slow-moving waggons set out at last along the city streets. They passed through the Aldgate and headed north up the Essex Great Road. The journey took most of that day. When finally the procession turned off the road into the tree-lined avenue leading to the Hall, it was with a mixture of excitement and exhaustion that the children leant out for their first view of the house. The day had been hot and the summer dust had risen in clouds from the roads. Every bone in their bodies ached from the

shaking, but it had been worth it for all the sights they had seen.

'Look there's a guard at the gatehouse,' called Hannah. The guard knew the driver and his halberd held across the leading horses was but in token of a search. Through the gatehouse the waggons creaked, past lines of buildings, on through another walled courtyard and at last the children caught their first sight of the house, its mellow brickwork gleaming orangy-red in the late afternoon sun. The house looked old though it had been finished but twenty years before. Past the West Wing the waggons moved on. Little did the children realise just how much of the house was still hidden from view.

All the servants from London and some from Ingatestone unloaded the waggons and then Hannah and Crispin were ready for their meat and drink. The male servants were sleeping in the lofts of the outbuildings and the female servants in the little garrets in the South Wing. Even though they were tired there was still much to be done before anyone was allowed to their beds.

As the day wore on and dusk settled over the tall chimneys of the Hall, Crispin began to wonder whether Master Kyme had forgotten his promise. It would not be surprising with so much on his mind. Yet Crispin was wrong. Late that evening, as Crispin was wearily stacking wood for the great kitchen fireplace, John Kyme came to find him. He beckoned him without a word and Crispin caught Hannah's eye as he followed him. Along passageways and up flights of stairs; sometimes it was just the tips of his gown that Crispin spotted disappearing round some corner of the house. At last he stopped outside a door and waited for the boy.

'Crispin, your parchment has indeed caused quite a stir.

Sir William has asked me to bring you to see him. Don't be nervous boy. Just answer his questions boldly. And you will find he is not alone.'

John Kyme knocked once on the door then held it open for him to enter.

Crispin had never seen so long a room in his life. It was panelled for all its length, with windows looking out over the orchard or into the courtyard on the other side. Portraits lined the walls and a pair of virginals stood under one of the windows. An enormous shovelboard stood in a corner. Crispin had played that game.

Despite the warm evening, there was a blazing log fire. Sir William was facing the door, sitting in a richly upholstered chair. In a similar chair with his back to Crispin sat another figure, looking remarkably like Sir William Petre. His gown and ruff were almost identical as was his medallion of office. When he turned so Crispin could see his face he saw he was several years younger.

Sir William beckoned Crispin nearer and John Kyme quietly closed the door as he went out.

'Master Crispin, it seems that a certain piece of parchment has given you a degree of trouble over these last two days. Well I hope it will comfort you to know that we are grateful to you for your help in bringing it to us, none more so than my friend Sir William Cecil.'

Crispin was visibly shaken. Was this the great Sir William Cecil, Chief advisor to Queen Elizabeth? Crispin had almost to pinch himself to believe that he, until two days ago a Bread Street apprentice, was now standing in the same room with two of the most powerful men in England.

Sir William Petre invited the boy to kneel by the fire where both men could see him.

'Would it surprise you if I told you that your 'beggar' was well known to me Master Crispin?' Secretary Cecil spoke slowly, emphasising the words. He smiled at the boy but his eyes held Crispin's as he spoke.

The parchment which fell into your hands was undoubtedly meant for mine, and the information it contains well – shall we say it is of considerable importance.' Cecil turned the parchment over so the cover was showing. 'You see by the writing on the outside, our beggar – I shall call him Bartholomew Smith for that is how we knew him – was about to send the note by means of a Thames waterman to Whitehall Palace. He did not quite have time to complete his instructions. He was . . . disturbed in the way you know only too well. The sign of the rose is now familiar to you I believe.

The two men glanced at one another before Cecil continued:

'Though you are but – what? – twelve years of age, I shall nevertheless entrust you with a secret, and you must promise me that nothing will persuade you to tell another soul. Do you promise boy?

'I promise sir.'

'Many wicked men would fain that our Queen were Queen no more. In Spain there smoulders a deep anger that England is no longer a Catholic country. In your beggar's note St James the Great is read as Spain. He also mentions the house in the Strand and that is the home of De Quadra the Spanish Ambassador. It is a rendezvous for conspirators who come and go using the back watergate to the river. There is nothing we can do but wait, and pounce like the fox when the time is right.

Sir William Petre, putting on his spectacles, joined in the conversation:

'Although many of the names on the list are known to us Crispin, we have no knowledge of your gentleman in blue.'

'And that is where you come in young Master.' Secretary Cecil looked hard at Crispin.' I must ask your help once more – in her Majesty's service this time. We are confident that this gentleman in blue as you call him, has been anxious that your parchment should not fall into our hands. He knows you have it, so must have followed you from Cheapside when Bartholomew Smith was killed.'

The two men were now standing, facing Crispin. Cecil spoke again.

'We believe the Queen is in danger. Our 'beggar' said as much in his note. We believe they aim to kidnap the Queen, or worse, and re-establish a Catholic on the throne. They will probably not act at Ingatestone but further along her progress route. We do not know where. Be on your guard for the man you described, but remember he may be dressed as a servant, or a waggon driver. You have seen his face only once, but if you see him again . . .'

'We must know straight away Crispin.' Sir William Petre

finished for him. 'Now off to bed with you.'

Cecil nodded once to the boy and then turned away. He picked up his glass of wine and sank into the chair again with a weary sigh.

That night Crispin's sleep was troubled in a different way. He felt within him a gnawing anxiety that the plot might succeed. How could he ever forgive himself if something dreadful happened to the Queen?

• • • • •

The next morning Crispin woke to a scene such as he could never have imagined. Though it was yet early, there were carpenters and bricklayers putting the final touches to the temporary buildings to house the hundreds of retainers that a royal progress brought with it. An honour on a house indeed, but an honour that could cause financial ruin. Elsewhere servants were already unloading the carts and waggons that seemed to arrive by the minute, loaded with ducks and young heron and cygnets from as far away as Kent and Ely. Sir William had a number of kind friends who were prepared to help him with the enormous quantities of food that would be needed for the three days of the Royal visit. Hogsheads of beer, baskets of oranges and pears and plums, quail and oysters and fresh salmon. All arrived and were speedily unloaded.

Crispin dressed and found his way down to the kitchen. He was glad Francis and Hannah were there with him. A hunk of bread was all the breakfast he could find that day.

'Get your head under the pump and wash some of the

sleep out of your eyes.' Francis gave him a friendly pat round the ear. Hannah was bubbling over with excitement.

'Master Willcocks the cook wants me to help in the kitchen to prepare the food for the Queen. I have lots of herbs to pick ... mint and hyssop and chervil and tarragon. I hope I can recognise them. And something called turnsole for the purple jellies!' She ran off in the direction of the herb garden.

Master Kyme came into the kitchen with his large leather book muttering to himself as he ticked the items on his seemingly endless list. '600 eggs, 14 dishes of butter at 7d a dish, 5 gallons of cream at 8d a gallon, 1 barrel of olives, half a peck of fine white salt, 200 oranges . . .' The list ran on for page after page. Crispin's wages were 6d a week and the cost of all this food made his head swim. John Kyme's voice trailed away as Crispin made for the pump. He took a sniff at himself as he went and was reminded that it was a good three months since he had taken a bath. Perhaps he would have one in honour of the Queen's visit, if he could find a tub anywhere.

The hours ticked by on the last day of preparations. In the grand rooms of the house Sir William's wife Lady Anne, sometimes helped by their four daughters, was making ready the Royal chambers. The wall hangings were in place and rose petals scattered to sweeten the air. Now all the finery they were to wear must be attended to. The Queen might have thousands of dresses to choose from but Lady Anne must not disgrace her husband nor must her daughters; nor their eleven year old son John who was more interested in his archery than meeting the Queen.

But during the hours of July 18th one visitor arrived at the

Hall who was much interested in meeting the Queen. He had discarded his blue doublet and hose for the grey marble of the Ingatestone livery. He intended to merge into the confusion of all that was happening and bide his moment.

CHAPTER SIX

Saturday 19th July 1561 dawned. The morning was as busy as the previous day. It seemed as if nothing would be ready, yet before noon the ripples of excitement around the Hall took on a different feel, less full of anxiety and more of eager expectation. They were ready. The great table was laid with the finest linen and silver. The mountains of food were reaching perfection. Being a fish day, royal sturgeon had been chosen. The joints of beef and roast duck and swan would await the following day.

Sir William and Lady Anne, their family and important guests were now in their finery, newly starched ruffs gleaming white against their throats. Master Kyme was still busy rushing from place to place checking his lists. Had they provided enough fodder for the hundreds of horses?

Master Willcocks the master cook from London knowing Her Majesty's sweet tooth had created his most fragrant and colourful sweetmeats and puddings for the Queen's delight. Custards, marchpanes, syllabubs, crystallized fruits, purple jellies, gilded gingerbread and kissing comfits to sweeten the breath.

Twelve o'clock approached.

'Crispin, the trumpet!' Hannah yelled at the top of her voice. A trumpeter on the roof of the Hall had spotted the plumes and uniforms of the great procession snaking its way through the green Essex countryside, approaching the lane leading to Ingatestone. All were in their positions. Nothing in the wonderful procession must be missed.

And now those on the ground could see the riders in their scarlet livery. Her servants were at the front of the procession followed by two of her guard. Then came her equerries, gentlemen servants of the Queen mounted on thoroughbreds and behind these her chamberlains, twenty in number. Then such of the Privy Council as were accompanying the Queen. Closest to Her Majesty rode Sir William Cecil.

'Look there's the Queen's coach.' An excited murmur broke out as the swaying plumes of the green and gold coach passed through the gatehouse arch, and a great cheer broke out from all sides of the court. Servants and ladies and gentlemen alike caught their first sight of the Queen. Bowing her head slightly, first to left then to right, acknowledging the cheers of her loyal subjects, Elizabeth Tudor, by the Grace of God Queen of England, had come to honour the house of one of her most trusted advisers.

In all her peacock glory, a gold and lace ruff framing the whole of her head like butterfly wings, she took Sir William's arm and stepped from the coach where it had drawn up in front of the oak doorway. The cheers reached a deafening climax as she turned to greet all around her. Sir William presented her first to Lady Anne and his children, then to his guests, and finally, representing all his servants, to John Kyme his Chief Steward.

Behind the royal coach came the Master of the Horse, the Maids of Honour and some fifty more of the Queen's Guard as well as numerous other servants. When the Queen's coach had been taken to its resting place, the horses unharnessed and the Queen escorted through the Screens Passage to the Great Hall, the procession of baggage waggons was still turning off the Essex Great Road a mile away.

John Kyme was quick to make sure that the kitchen servants wasted not a minute more than they should.

Crispin and Hannah and the many others engaged in preparing the Queen's first meal were soon hard at work amidst the heat and steam of the kitchens. Stewed carp and pike with 'high Dutch' sauce disappeared in the direction of the Great Hall to accompany the sturgeon. For the servants there were dishes of turnip and pumpkin, carrots and leeks to eke out their fish, and boiled puddings and frumenty bubbling away for later in their meal. Gallon upon gallon of beer and ale and wine disappeared down thirsty throats.

Musicians played to accompany the Queen's feasting and though it was said Her Majesty had but a small appetite, she did full justice to the delicacies that Ingatestone had provided for her, as did the hundreds of other mouths. Servants tried to appear calm as they transported the gleaming silver trays and dishes to the royal table. Crispin and Francis were two of the many who tried to keep up with the never-ending washing in the wooden tubs, as dish after dish returned.

'I hope there's enough left for us to try the food.' Crispin looked longingly at the mouthwatering fare passing his way.

'Never fear lad,' said Francis, 'I have not known a feast yet where every scrap is eaten. You'll get you first taste of royal sturgeon yet.'

• • • • •

The day wore on. Her Majesty was taken to the chambers set aside for her private use to rest and recover from her journey.

It wasn't until evening that Crispin and Hannah had their first chance to meet and talk. Crispin was nervous yet secretive following his promise to Secretary Cecil. Throughout the day every new face coming towards him had made his heart beat faster. He told Hannah all he dared.

'Do they think the gentleman in blue is going to appear at Ingatestone? Hannah's eyes showed her alarm.

'Yes, but he won't be the gentleman in blue anymore. He could look like anyone.' I have imagined seeing him at least twenty times.

'But what if he finds you first Crispin, you know what happened to the old beggar. Please be careful.'

Crispin was touched by her concern. His words tried not to betray how scared he felt.

'Don't worry, I can look after myself.' Hannah remembering the sight of Crispin in the lane near St. Paul's rather doubted it.

• • • • •

But nothing out of the ordinary happened and the next two days of the Queen's visit went past in a fury of activity. Never had either of the children seen so much food. Dish upon dish was prepared for the royal table. It was non-stop eating. Joints of lamb and beef and venison and golden pasties passed between the kitchens and the Great Hall, or at times to the smaller dining chamber where the Queen ate privately. All her food had to be tasted first, just to be sure. In between were the entertainments: falconry which the Queen loved, a 'banquet' in the grounds, and a wonderful Masque with acting and music. Every evening there was dancing, pavans and galliards and the daring La Volta. Her Majesty danced well.

In her more private moments, gambling at cards and backgammon passed the pleasant hours between eating, whilst the army of servants prepared the next feast. Sir William Cecil had scarcely seen Her Majesty more relaxed and happy. Behind the pleasures of the feasting some of her courtiers grumbled at the inconvenience of the temporary quarters which were their lot, yet they dared not risk Her Majesty's displeasure in not attending upon her progress.

Sunday passed into Monday and the climax of feasting and festivities was reached. But not once did Crispin's anxiety abate. It was only the activity of the days that released his mind from the shadow of the gentleman in blue. He became in the boy's thoughts some devil watching him and waiting to seize the moment for his evil. But Tuesday morning did dawn, with a grey mist hanging over the roofs of the hall. It was the morning Her Majesty was due to take her leave of Sir William and move to her next residence at New Hall near Chelmsford. The Petre family's duty was all but done.

Crispin had almost stopped searching every stranger's face that came towards him and imagined that even Secretary Cecil had been mistaken. The panic was at last subsiding and the pace of life returning to normal. Crispin had been given the job of fetching two small barrels of ale from the beer cellar. He had left Hannah outside in the walled garden. He was just about to enter the door leading to the cellar when a man ran round a corner almost colliding with him. For a brief moment their eyes met and although the man was dressed in the same way as all the other servants at Ingatestone, the face that Crispin saw with its black, trimmed beard was the face of the man who had 'accidentally' tripped him. Crispin could not hide his brief recognition and the man saw it. He cursed and roughly clapped his hand over the boy's mouth. The man's knee was in Crispin's back pushing him forward and before he could resist he had been bundled into the cellar and thrown against the barrels.

'So it seems as if our paths have crossed again boy. You

have caused me a great deal of worry and anxiety, a great deal. I believe you have a document which belongs to me. I should very much like it back.'

'I haven't got it any more.' Crispin despite his panic knew he must not give the man a hint that Secretary Cecil had seen the parchment and the list of names.

'You haven't got it. Then pray what have you done with it.' The man's hands were roughly at the boy's collar, lifting him slightly. 'Shown it to your important friends perhaps?'

'No I threw it away. I can't read.' The mans eyes flickered with anger and he cut the boy hard across his face with the side of his hand. He was weighing up in his mind a number of possibilities. If the boy were telling the truth then perhaps all was safe after all, but if he was lying? Would there be time for a little gentle . . . persuasion, to find out?'

'There is no one will hear your shouts down here boy, but just in case,' and he tore a strip of cloth used for dusting the barrels and tied it firmly over his mouth. He found two pieces of rope beneath the small window and tied the boy's hands and feet. He slammed the door shut and turned the key.

It must have been half an hour when his captor and another man, also dressed in Sir William's livery, returned. Checking the passageway they carried Crispin and bundled him into an extremely small room that seemed to be tucked into the wall.

'That should keep him out of the way for as long as we need.' The bearded man was able to ignore the boy as if he was of no further danger to them. He had convinced himself that their activities must be undiscovered.

'Is everything arranged?'

'Yes,' the second man replied. The trees are held by

ropes. When the royal coach is between the trees the ropes will be cut and the trees will fall and block the path of the guards behind and in front. Before they realize what has happened Queen Bess will be our prisoner and on her way across country by horseback. We will negotiate for her life and before long will have a Catholic country again.'

Crispin listened with horror and realised that unless he could somehow break free from this prison the plan might very well succeed.

The door, part of the panelling, slammed shut and from where he sat Crispin knew that the sounds of jingling harnesses meant the royal procession was forming up. His wriggling could loosen nothing.

He heard the trumpet in the distance as he had heard it when the Queen arrived. He knew that Sir William and Lady Anne would once again be lined up to take their leave of Her Majesty. He knew Hannah would be desperately worried. The cheering reached his ears and he pictured the leading horses passing through the gatehouse.

Bound hand and foot and gagged, he hopped about the room. It seemed that hours had passed but in truth it was but minutes, when he had the idea of throwing himself against the panelled door. If he could not break it, then at least someone might hear him.

It was about his tenth attempt that a miracle happened. Instead of hitting the door, the weight of his body hit the section of wall to the right and some hidden mechanism was jarred into action; the door burst open and he was catapulted into a small chamber. A startled maid let out a scream as some 'devil' white with dust and trussed like a chicken burst out of the wall at her feet. When she had recovered she first undid the boy's gag and then his ropes.

'Mistress Hannah,' he cried, 'do you know where Mistress Hannah is?'

'Why all the servants have just returned to the kitchens and sculleries. There is much work to . . .'

Crispin didn't listen to another word. He ran along the passageway and was round the corner before the astonished maid could gather her wits.

Hannah was so delighted to see Crispin again, she didn't stop to ask questions. He grabbed her by the hand and they sped out through the door and across the lawns.

'Hi you can't . . .' The old gardener was speechless with rage as these young servants ran across the parterre towards the strangers' stable. Then they heard the whinny of a horse from just inside the gatehouse and scrambled up the wall to look. Several horses were ready saddled, waiting for Sir William's friends to depart. Only a stable boy was with them and he was too surprised to realise what was happening, but as they mounted and cantered through the gatehouse arch the horsekeeper saw them. His face was furious as he chased them past the new granary.

'Horse-thieves!' he yelled to the guards at the gatehouse and their reactions were swift. Neither of the children were good riders, but both had ridden before. The powerful horses took charge and Hannah and Crispin clung tightly, not daring to look behind for signs of the pursuit they knew would come.

Luckily the road was easy to guess, from the villagers who stood in groups, still recovering from the marvels they had seen. It was said that her Majesty never took thought for her own safety when her loyal subjects wished to greet her, and would stop her coach to please them.

Clouds of dust were kicked up by the speeding hooves,

as the children rode in desperation to prevent a tragedy they did not really understand. It seemed an age before Crispin caught sight of the dragging baggage waggons and called behind him to Hannah. The guards were fierce in trying to prevent their getting near the Queen's coach, and one of them grabbed at Crispin's bridle and unseated him. He fell to the ground. Hannah leapt off her own horse and ran over to him, as he struggled to his feet.

'We must see Master Cecil. The Queen is in danger.' The anxiety on the boy's face almost persuaded the guard that Crispin was telling the truth but then the cry of 'horse thieves' rang out clearly along the road behind them. Crispin seized his chance. He wriggled out of the soldier's grasp and ran alongside the slow-moving procession. With Hannah close behind him, he dodged in and out of the waggons and was only stopped when he was within sight of the Queen's coach. Hearing the yells, a familiar face looked out of the coach mearest to him.

'Release those children, I can vouch for them.' Secretary Cecil's orders were obeyed.

Out of the corner of his eye Crispin saw another familiar face. His guise was again different but Crispin would have recognised him anywhere. The eyes were dark with a blazing anger.

'There's the man sir!' Crispin startled Cecil by his yell but the Secretary acted instantly. Crispin never knew whether the dagger in the man's hand was for him or whether desperation had made him choose a yet more dreadful alternative to his plan. Guards were on him like wild dogs and he was pinned to the ground.

• • • • •

And with the leader of the plot under guard, a party of mounted soldiers set off in the direction of Chelmsford, galloping along the grassy slopes bordering the road. So silent was their arrival at the wooded hollow chosen by the would-be kidnappers, that after one fierce volley of gunfire, the plotters were arrested.

• • • • •

The royal procession was still standing at its unplanned resting place. Sir William Cecil with a look of great relief on his face had allowed himself a tankard of beer. Behind him, the sweat still sticky on their faces, stood Crispin and Hannah.

One of the equerries from Her Majesty's escort came up and whispered something to Secretary Cecil.

'It seems that the two of you are to have your first royal audience.'

Crispin and Hannah could hardly understand what they were hearing. Crispin thought of Thomas and Sarah. They would never believe this.

'You mean we . . .'

'Yes, it seems that Her Majesty would like to thank you in person.'

'But we can't . . . look at our state.'

Hannah was overwhelmed at the thought of meeting Her Majesty, looking as she did, her skirt and shoes covered in mud.

'You would not refuse her Majesty? The Queen does understand that you have ridden rather fast to see her!'

Cecil smiled at the children and with difficulty they tried to smile back. Avoiding one another's eyes, they followed the equerry through the woodland clearing to where the plumes of the royal coach fluttered in the warm afternoon breeze.

AUTHOR'S NOTE

The background to UNDER THE ROSE is factual. Although the details of this plot are fictitious, a number of serious attempts on the Queen's life were made. She did have her 'secret service', organized by Sir Francis Walsingam, a little later in her reign.

The descriptions of Sir William Petre, his London house in Aldersgate and of Queen Elizabeth's visit to Ingatestone are based on fact. For this background material I am much indebted to Dr F.G. Emmison the eminent former Archivist of Essex, author of 'Tudor Secretary', a study of Sir William Petre.

To the present Lord Petre I am very grateful both for allowing me to include his Tudor ancestor in the story and for his support for the book and the teachers' pack which accompanies it.

I should like to record my thanks to the staff of the Guildhall Library, London, for answering specific questions relating to Tudor London and to Mr Ian Mason of the Essex Record Office for his help. I also acknowledge as a source Peggy Millar's 'Life in Elizabethan London'.

Finally, as the idea for the story has arisen from a school experiment in teaching Tudor history via a real house, Ingatestone Hall, and a real Tudor family, that of Sir William Petre, I acknowledge the help and support of my colleague Mr Mike Pond, Headteacher of Kinsale Middle School, Norwich.

PLACES TO VISIT

Ann Hathaway's Cottage, Shottery. Warwickshire.

Audley End, Saffron Walden, Essex.

Burghley House, Stamford Baron, Northamptonshire.

Elizabethan House Museum, Great Yarmouth, Norfolk.

Hampton Court Palace, London.

Hardwick Hall, Derbyshire.

·Hatfield House, Hatfield, Hertfordshire

Ingatestone Hall, Chelmsford, Essex.

Kentwell Hall, Long Melford, Suffolk: (Tudor Re-Creations each summer)

Kirby Hall, Gretton, Northamptonshire.

Knole, Sevenoaks, Kent.

Layer Marney, Colchester, Essex.

Little Moreton Hall, Congleton, Cheshire.

Longleat, Horningsham, Wiltshire.

Mary Rose Museum, Portsmouth, Hampshire.

Montacute, Somerset.

Museum of London.

Paycocke's House, Coggeshall, Essex.

Penshurst Place, Penshurst, Kent.

Strangers Hall Museum, Norwich, Norfolk.

Sutton Place, Shalford, Surrey.